OVERCOMING DEPRESSION

A GUIDE AND A CURE TO DEPRESSION

BY TAYLOR GRANT

Presentation:

Part 1.   MEANING OF   DEPRESSION

Part 2.   HOW BIOLOGY IS RELATED TO DEPRESSION

Part 3.   DEPRESSION SYMPTOMS

Part 4.   TREATMENT FOR DEPRESSION

Part 5.   NORMAL CURE AND WAY OF LIFE TIPS EXERCISE

Part 6.   FORESTALLING DEPRESSION

Conclusion:

Presentation

Depression is a complicated illness. Nobody knows precisely very thing purposes it, yet it can occur for different reasons. Certain individuals have misery during a serious clinical disease. Others might have melancholy with life changes like a move or the demise of a friend or family member. Still others have a family background of sadness. The individuals who truly do may have misery and feel overpowered with pity and dejection for not a really obvious explanation.

Everybody can feel miserable or overpowered on occasion. In any case, melancholy is a persistent sensation of vacancy, bitterness, or failure to feel delight that might seem to occur for not a great explanation. It is particular from sadness and different feelings an individual might feel following troublesome life altering situations.

It is a continuous issue, not a passing one. While there are various sorts of discouragement, the most well-known one is significant burdensome problem. It comprises of episodes during which the side effects keep going for something like fourteen days.

Discouragement can keep going for a little while, months, or years. For some individuals, a persistent disease improves and afterward backslides.

Part 1.

MEANING OF DEPRESSION

Depression is a mind-set jumble that causes relentless sensations of pity, vacancy, and loss of delight. Not quite the same as the state of mind vacillations individuals routinely experience as a piece of life.

Significant life altering situations, like mourning or the passing of a task, can set off misery. Be that as it may, gloom is particular from the pessimistic sentiments an individual may briefly have in light of a troublesome life altering situation.

Wretchedness frequently endures despite a difference in conditions and causes sentiments that are extraordinary, persistent, and not corresponding to an individual's conditions.

The Primary Drivers Of Depression

There are loads of things that can expand the opportunity of despondency like maltreatment, physical, sexual, or psychological mistreatment can make one more powerless against wretchedness further down the road and furthermore such with others, for example,

Age: Individuals who are old are at higher gamble of despondency. That can be exacerbated by different variables, for example, living alone and having an absence of social help.

Certain medications :A few medications, for example, isotretinoin (used to treat skin break out), the antiviral medication interferon-alpha, and corticosteroids, can expand your gamble of despondency.

Struggle: Melancholy in somebody who has the natural weakness to it might result from private issues or questions with relatives or companions.

Passing or a misfortune: Trouble or pain after the demise or loss of a friend or family member, however normal, can build the gamble of sadness.

Orientation: Ladies are about two times as logical as men to become discouraged. Nobody's certain why. The hormonal changes that ladies go through at various seasons of their lives might assume a part.

Qualities: A family background of despondency might build the gamble. It's felt that downturn is a perplexing quality, importance there are most likely various qualities that each apply little impacts, instead of a solitary quality that adds to illness risk. The hereditary qualities of discouragement, as most mental issues, are not quite as basic or direct as in absolutely hereditary illnesses like Huntington's chorea or cystic fibrosis.

Significant occasions: Even great occasions like beginning a new position, graduating, or getting hitched can prompt misery. So can moving, losing an employment or pay, getting separated, or resigning. Be that as it may, the disorder of clinical misery is rarely only a "ordinary" reaction to unpleasant life altering situations.

Other individual issues: Issues, for example, social disconnection because of other psychological maladjustments or being projected out of a family or gathering can add to the gamble of creating clinical despondency.

Difficult diseases: Some of the time, sorrow occurs alongside a significant sickness or might be set off by another ailment.
Substance abuse. Almost 30% of individuals with substance abuse issues likewise have major or clinical despondency. Regardless of whether medications or liquor briefly encourage you, they at last will bother gloom.

Part 2.

HOW BIOLOGY IS RELATED TO DEPRESSION

Scientists have noted contrasts in the cerebrums of individuals who have clinical discouragement contrasted and the people who don't. For example, the hippocampus, a little piece of the cerebrum that is crucial to the capacity of recollections, seems, by all accounts, to be more modest in certain individuals with a background marked by misery than in those who've never been discouraged. A more modest hippocampus has less serotonin receptors. Serotonin is one of many mind synthetic substances known as synapses that permit correspondence across circuits that associate the cerebrum areas engaged with handling feelings.

Researchers don't have any idea why the hippocampus might be more modest in certain individuals with wretchedness. A few specialists have observed that the pressure chemical cortisol is created in overabundance in discouraged individuals. These examiners accept that cortisol has a harmful or "contracting" impact on the improvement of the hippocampus. A few specialists figure discouraged individuals might be just brought into the world with a more modest hippocampus and are subsequently disposed to have wretchedness. There are numerous other mind districts, and pathways between unambiguous locales, remembered to be engaged with despondency, and logical, no single cerebrum design or pathway seecompletely represents clinical sadness.

One thing is sure: Depression is a complicated sickness with many contributing elements. The most recent sweeps and investigations of mind construction and capability propose that antidepressants can apply "neurotrophic impacts," implying that they can assist with supporting nerve cells, keep them from kicking the bucket, and permit them to frame more grounded associations that endure organic anxieties. As researchers gain a superior comprehension of the reasons for sorrow, wellbeing experts will actually want to improve "customized" analyze and, thus, recommend more compelling treatment plans.

How Genetics Is Linked To The Risk Of Depression

We realize that downturn can once in a while run in families. This recommends that there's basically a halfway hereditary connection to despondency. Youngsters, kin, and guardians of individuals with serious wretchedness are fairly bound to have sorrow than are individuals from everybody. Different qualities connecting with each other in unique ways most likely add to the different sorts of sadness that spat families. However in spite of the proof of a family connect to despondency, it is impossible that there is a solitary "gloom" quality, yet rather, numerous qualities that each contribute little impacts toward sadness when they communicate with the climate.

How Certain Medications Really do Cause Sorrow

In specific individuals, medications might prompt misery. For instance, prescriptions like barbiturates, benzodiazepines, and the skin break out drug isotretinoin (previously sold as Accutane, presently Absorica, Amnesteem, Claravis, Myorisan, Zenatane) have some of the time been connected with despondency, particularly in more seasoned individuals. Moreover, drugs like corticosteroids, narcotics (codeine, morphine), and anticholinergics taken to ease stomach squeezing can here and there cause changes and vacillations in temperament. Indeed, even pulse prescriptions called beta-blockers have been connected to wretchedness.

The Connection Among Misery And Constant Ailment

In certain individuals, a constant sickness causes discouragement. An ongoing sickness is a disease that goes on for quite a while and typically can't be restored totally. Notwithstanding, constant ailments can frequently be controlled through diet, work out, way of life propensities, and certain prescriptions. A few instances of ongoing sicknesses that might cause discouragement are diabetes, coronary illness, joint pain, kidney infection, HIV and Helps, lupus, and various sclerosis (MS). Hypothyroidism may likewise prompt discouraged sentiments.
Specialists accept that treating the downturn may at times likewise assist the existing together clinical ailment with moving along.

Wretchedness Is Connected to Ongoing Agony

At the point when agony waits for weeks to months, it's classified "constant." In addition to the fact that ongoing aggravation harms, it upsets your rest, your capacity to practice and be dynamic, your connections, and your efficiency at work. Could you at any point perceive how ongoing agony may likewise leave you feeling miserable, disengaged, and discouraged?

There is help for constant agony and discouragement. A diverse program of medication, psychotherapy, support gatherings, and more can assist you with dealing with your aggravation, facilitate your downturn, and get your life in the groove again.

Sorrow That Frequently Happen With Distress

Melancholy is a typical, ordinary reaction to misfortune. Misfortunes that might prompt melancholy incorporate the passing or detachment of a friend or family member, cutback of an employment, demise or loss of a cherished pet, or quite a few different changes throughout everyday life, like separation, turning into an "unfilled nester," or retirement.

Anybody can encounter melancholy and misfortune, yet not every person will encounter clinical discouragement, which contrasts from sadness in that downturn includes a scope of different side effects like sensations of low self-esteem, pessimistic contemplations about the future, and self destruction, while distress includes sensations of vacancy, misfortune and yearning for a friend or family member, with an unblemished ability to feel joy. Every individual is remarkable by they way they adapt to these sentiments.

However despondency and melancholy offer a few elements, misery is not the same as sorrow felt in the wake of losing a friend or family member or pity felt after a horrible life altering situation. Discouragement normally includes self-hatred or a deficiency of confidence, while misery commonly doesn't.
In sadness, good feelings and cheerful recollections of the departed ordinarily go with sensations of close to home agony. In significant burdensome problem, the sensations of trouble are consistent.
 Misery is named a mind-set jumble. It could be depicted as sensations of bitterness, misfortune, or outrage that obstruct an individual's regular exercises.

It's likewise genuinely considered normal. Information from the Habitats for Infectious prevention appraises that 18.5 percent of grown-ups had side effects of wretchedness in some random 2-week time frame.

Individuals experience sorrow in various ways. It might disrupt your day to day work, bringing about lost time and lower efficiency. It can likewise impact connections and some persistent medical issue.

Conditions That Can Get Worse Due To Depression Include:

joint inflammation
asthma
cardiovascular illness
malignant growth
diabetes
heftiness

It's vital to understand that inclination down on occasion is an ordinary piece of life. Miserable and disturbing occasions happen to everybody. Be that as it may, assuming that you're feeling down or sad consistently, you could be managing despondency. Gloom is viewed as a serious ailment that can seek more terrible without legitimate treatment.

Part 3.

DEPRESSION SYMPTOMS

Misery can be in excess of a steady mindset of pity or feeling "blue. Significant misery can cause different side effects. A few influence your mind-set and others influence your body. Side effects may likewise be continuous or come and go.

General Signs And Side Effects

Not every person with wretchedness will encounter similar side effects. Side effects can fluctuate in seriousness, how frequently they occur, and how lengthy they last.
Assuming you experience a portion of the accompanying signs and side effects of

melancholy virtually consistently for no less than about fourteen days, you might be living with discouragement:

Syptoms are:

feeling miserable, restless, or "void"
feeling sad, useless, and skeptical
crying a ton
feeling irritated, irritated, or irate
loss of interest in leisure activities and interests you once appreciated
diminished energy or weariness
trouble focusing, recollecting, or deciding
moving or talking all the more leisurely
trouble dozing, early daytime arousing, or sleeping late
hunger or weight changes
ongoing actual agony with no unmistakable reason that seeks worse with treatment (migraines, throbs or torments, stomach related issues, cramps)

considerations of death, self destruction,
self-damage, or self destruction
endeavors
The side effects of melancholy can be
capable distinctively among guys,
females, adolescents, and youngsters.

Guys might encounter side effects
connected with their:
mind-set, like indignation, forcefulness,
crabbiness, nervousness, or fretfulness
close to home prosperity, like inclination
vacant, miserable, or irredeemable
conduct, for example, loss of interest,
done finding delight in most loved
exercises, feeling tired effectively,
considerations of self destruction,
drinking unnecessarily, utilizing drugs, or
participating in high-risk exercises
sexual interest, like diminished sexual
longing or absence of sexual execution
mental capacities, for example,
powerlessness to think, trouble finishing

responsibilities, or postponed reactions
during discussions
rest designs, like a sleeping disorder,
fretful rest, inordinate drowsiness, or not
staying asleep for the entire evening
actual prosperity, like weariness, agonies,
migraine, or stomach related issues.

Females might encounter side effects
connected with their:
mind-set, like touchiness
profound prosperity, for example, feeling
miserable or unfilled, restless, or sad
conduct, like loss of interest in exercises,
pulling out from social commitment, or
considerations of self destruction
mental capacities, like reasoning or
talking all the more leisurely
rest designs, for example, trouble staying
asleep from sundown to sunset, waking
early, or dozing excessively
actual prosperity, for example,
diminished energy, more prominent
weariness, changes in craving, weight
changes, throbs, torment, cerebral pains,
or expanded cramps

Youngsters might encounter side effects
connected with their:

temperament, like peevishness, outrage,
quick changes in mind-set, or crying
close to home prosperity, like sensations
of ineptitude (e.g., "I can do nothing
right") or misery, crying, or extraordinary
bitterness
conduct, for example, causing problems at
the everyday schedule to go to class,
keeping away from companions or kin,
considerations of death or self
destruction, or self-hurt
mental capacities, for example, trouble
concentrating, decrease in school
execution, or changes in grades
rest designs, for example, trouble dozing
or resting excessively
actual prosperity, like loss of energy,
stomach related issues, changes in
craving, or weight reduction or gain.

Depression Causes

There are a few potential reasons for despondency. They can go from organic to fortuitous normal causes include:

Cerebrum science: There might be a substance lopsidedness in pieces of the mind that oversee temperament, considerations, rest, hunger, and conduct in individuals who have sorrow.

Chemical levels: Changes in female chemicals estrogen and progesterone during various timeframes like during the monthly cycle, post pregnancy period, perimenopause, or menopause may all raise an individual's gamble for sorrow. Family ancestry. You're at a higher gamble for creating despondency on the off chance that you have a family background of misery or another mind-set jumble.

Youth injury: A few occasions influence the manner in which your body responds to fear and distressing circumstances.

Cerebrum structure: There's a more serious gamble for melancholy in the event that the cerebrum of your mind is less dynamic. Nonetheless, researchers couldn't say whether this occurs previously or after the beginning of burdensome side effects.

Ailments: Certain circumstances might put you at higher gamble, for example, constant sickness, a sleeping disorder, persistent torment, Parkinson's illness, stroke, coronary episode, and disease. Substance use. A past filled with substance or liquor abuse can influence your gamble.

Torment: Individuals who feel profound or persistent actual agony for extensive stretches of time are fundamentally more likelyTrusted Source to foster sorrow.

Risk Variables

Risk factors for depression can be biochemical, clinical, social, hereditary, or incidental. Normal gamble factors include:

Sex. The pervasiveness of significant gloom is two times as high in females as in guys.

Hereditary qualities. You have an expanded gamble of despondency on the off chance that you have a family background of it.

Financial status. Financial status, including monetary issues and saw low economic wellbeing, can expand your gamble of melancholy.

Certain drugs. Certain medications including a few sorts of hormonal contraception, corticosteroids, and beta-blockers might be related with an expanded gamble of discouragement.

Lack of vitamin D. Studies have connected burdensome side effects to low degrees of vitamin D.

Substance abuse. Around 21% of individuals who have a substance use jumble likewise experience sadness.

Clinical sicknesses. Discouragement is related with other persistent clinical sicknesses. Individuals with coronary illness are about two times as to have discouragement as individuals who don't, while up to 1 of every 4 individuals with disease may likewise encounter gloom.

Part 4.

TREATMENT FOR DEPRESSION

You may effectively oversee side effects with one type of treatment, or you might find that a mix of medicines works best. It's not unexpected to join clinical medicines and way of life treatments, including the accompanying:

Prescriptions:

Specific serotonin reuptake inhibitors (SSRIs)
SSRIs are the most regularly recommended stimulant drugs and will more often than not make not many side impacts. They treat discouragement by

expanding the accessibility of the synapse serotonin in your mind.

SSRIs ought not be taken with specific medications including monoamine oxidase inhibitors (MAOIs) and now and again thioridazine or Orap (pimozide). Individuals who are pregnant ought to converse with their medical care experts about the dangers of taking SSRIs during pregnancy. You ought to likewise utilize alert assuming you have restricted point glaucoma.

Instances of SSRIs incorporate citalopram (Celexa), escitalopram (Lexapro), fluvoxamine (Luvox), paroxetine (Paxil, Paxil XR, Pexeva), and sertraline (Zoloft). Serotonin and norepinephrine reuptake inhibitors (SNRIs)

SNRIs treat discouragement by expanding how much the synapses serotonin and norepinephrine in your cerebrum.

SNRIs ought not be taken with MAOIs. You ought to utilize alert in the event that you have liver or kidney issues, or limited point glaucoma.

Instances of SNRIs incorporate

Desvenlafaxine (Pristiq, Khedezla), duloxetine (Cymbalta, Irenka), levomilnacipran (Fetzima), milnacipran (Savella), and venlafaxine (Effexor XR).

Tricyclic and Tetracyclic Antidepressants

Tricyclic antidepressants (TCAs) and tetracyclic antidepressants (TECAs) treat sorrow by expanding how much the synapses serotonin and norepinephrine in your mind.

TCAs can cause more incidental effects than SSRIs or SNRIs. Try not to take TCAs or TECAs with MAOIs. Use with alert on the off chance that you have slender point glaucoma.

Instances Of Tricyclic ;
antidepressants incorporate amitriptyline
(Elavil), doxepin (Sinequan), imipramine
(Tofranil), trimipramine (Surmontil),
desipramine (Norpramin), nortriptyline
(Pamelor, Aventyl), and protriptyline
(Vivactil).

Abnormal Antidepressants

Noradrenaline and dopamine reuptake
inhibitors (NDRIs)
These medications can treat sorrow by
expanding the degrees of dopamine and
noradrenaline in your mind.

Instances of NDRIs incorporate
bupropion (Wellbutrin)
Monoamine oxidase inhibitors (MAOIs)
MAOIs treat misery by expanding the
degrees of norepinephrine, serotonin,

dopamine, and tyramine in your cerebrum.

Because of incidental effects and wellbeing concerns MAOIs are not the best option for treating psychological well-being problems. They are regularly utilized provided that different meds are ineffective at treating sorrow.

Instances of MAOIs incorporate isocarboxazid (Marplan), phenelzine (Nardil), selegiline (Emsam), tranylcypromine (Parnate).

N-methyl-D-aspartate (NDMA) adversaries treat wretchedness by expanding levels of glutamate in the mind. Glutamate is a synapse accepted to be engaged with sadness.
NMDA adversaries are utilized exclusively in patients who have not had

accomplishment with other upper medicines.

The FDA has supported one NDMA medicine, esketamine(Spravato), for the treatment of discouragement.

Esketamine is a nasal shower that is just accessible through a limited program called Spravato REMS.

Patients might encounter sleepiness and separation (trouble with consideration, judgment, and thinking) subsequent to taking the drug. Therefore, esketamine is controlled in a medical services setting where a medical care proficient can screen for sedation and separation.

Each sort of drug that is utilized to treat wretchedness has advantages and likely dangers.

Psychotherapy

Talking with a specialist can assist you with mastering abilities to adapt to pessimistic sentiments. You may likewise profit from family or gathering treatment meetings.

Psychotherapy, otherwise called "talk treatment," is the point at which an individual addresses a prepared specialist to distinguish and figure out how to adapt to the elements that add to their emotional well-being condition, like sadness. Psychotherapy has been demonstrated to be a viable treatment in further developing side effects in individuals with despondency and other mental issues. Psychotherapy is much of the time utilized close by drug treatment. There are various kinds of psychotherapy, and certain individuals answer preferred to one sort over another.

Mental conduct treatment (CBT)
In mental conduct treatment (CBT), a specialist will work with you to reveal undesirable examples of thought and recognize how they might be causing unsafe ways of behaving, responses, and convictions about yourself.

Persuasive conduct treatment (DBT): Rationalistic conduct treatment (DBT) is like CBT, however puts a particular accentuation on approval, or tolerating awkward contemplations, sentiments, and ways of behaving, rather than battling them. The hypothesis is that by dealing with your hurtful considerations or feelings, you can acknowledge that change is conceivable and make a recuperation arrangement.

Psychodynamic treatment : This is a type of talk treatment intended to assist you with better comprehension and adapt to your everyday life. Psychodynamic treatment depends on the possibility that your present-day the truth is molded by your oblivious, adolescence encounters. Here of treatment, your advisor will help you reflect and analyze your experience growing up and encounters to help you comprehend and adapt to your life.

Light treatment: Openness to portions of white light can assist with managing your mind-set and further develop side effects of sorrow. Light treatment is ordinarily utilized in occasional full of feeling problem, which is currently called significant burdensome issue with occasional example.

Electroconvulsive treatment (ECT): This utilizes electrical flows to incite a seizure, and has been displayed to assist individuals with clinical wretchedness. It's utilized in individuals with extreme melancholy or discouragement that is impervious to different medicines or energizer drugs.
During an ECT methodology, you'll get a sedative specialist which will make it lights-out time for you for roughly 5 to 10 minutes.

Your medical services proficient will put cardiovascular checking cushions on your chest and four anodes on unambiguous region of your head. They will then, at that point, convey short electrical heartbeats for a couple of moments. You will neither writhe nor feel the electrical flow and will stir around 5 to 10 minutes after treatment.

Secondary effects incorporate migraines, sickness, muscle throbs and irritation, and disarray or bewilderment. Patients may likewise foster memory issues, however these generally dwell in the long stretches of time after treatment.

Elective treatments: Get some information about elective treatments for gloom. Many individuals decide to utilize elective treatments close by customary psychotherapy and drug. A few models include:

Contemplation. Stress, uneasiness, and outrage are triggers of sorrow, however reflection can assist with meaningfully impacting the manner in which your mind answers these feelings. Concentrates on demonstrate the way that contemplation practices can assist with further developing side effects of despondency and lower your possibilities of a downturn backslide.

Needle therapy: Needle therapy is a type of conventional Chinese medication that might end up being useful to facilitate a few side effects of misery. During needle therapy, a specialist utilizes needles to animate specific regions in the body to treat a scope of conditions. Research recommends that needle therapy might help clinical medicines work better and might be essentially as compelling as directing.

Part 5.

NORMAL CURE AND WAY OF LIFE TIPS EXERCISE

Go for the gold of active work 3 to 5 days every week. Exercise can expand your body's creation of endorphins, which are chemicals that work on your mind-set.

Keep away from liquor and substance use Drinking liquor or abusing substances might encourage you for a smidgen. Be that as it may, over the long haul, these substances can aggravate melancholy.

Figure Out How To Draw Certain Lines

Feeling overpowered can demolish nervousness and misery side effects. Defining limits in your expert and individual life can assist you with feeling far improved.

Deal With Yourself:
You can likewise further develop side effects of sorrow by dealing with yourself. This incorporates getting a lot of rest, eating a solid eating regimen, keeping away from pessimistic individuals, and taking part in pleasant exercises.
Now and again wretchedness doesn't answer prescription. Your medical care proficient may suggest other therapy choices in the event that your side effects get worse.

Supplements:
A few sorts of enhancements might affect misery side effects.

5-hydroxytryptophan (5-HTP) may bring serotonin steps up in the mind, which could ease side effects. Your body makes this substance when you consume tryptophan, a structure block of protein. Nonetheless, more investigations are required.

Omega-3 Unsaturated Fats:
These fundamental fats are mean quite a bit to neurological turn of events and mind wellbeing. Adding omega-3 enhancements to your eating regimen might assist with decreasing wretchedness side effects. Nonetheless, there is some clashing proof and more examination is required.

Continuously converse with your primary care physician prior to taking enhancements, as they might communicate with different drugs or make adverse consequences.

Nutrients:

Nutrients are mean a lot to many physical processes. Research proposes two nutrients are particularly helpful for facilitating side effects of wretchedness: Vitamin B: B-12 and B-6 are fundamental to mind wellbeing. At the point when your vitamin B levels are low, your gamble for creating misery might be higher.

Vitamin D: Once in a while called the daylight nutrient, vitamin D is significant for mind, heart, and bone wellbeing. There may beTrusted Source a connection between lack of vitamin D and melancholy, yet more exploration is required.

Numerous spices, enhancements, and nutrients guarantee to assist with facilitating side effects of wretchedness, however most haven't demonstrated the fact that they are viable in clinical exploration.

Melancholy Test:
There is certainly not a solitary test to analyze wretchedness. However, your medical services supplier can make a conclusion in view of your side effects and a mental assessment.
By and large, they'll pose a progression of inquiries about your:

Temperaments
Hunger
Rest design
Action level
Considerations
Since discouragement can be connected to other medical issues, your medical care proficient may likewise lead an actual assessment and request blood work.
Some of the time thyroid issues or a lack of vitamin D can set off side effects of melancholy.

Disregarding side effects of depression is significant not. On the off chance that your temperament doesn't improve or deteriorates, look for clinical assistance. Wretchedness is a serious emotional well-being disease with the potential for inconveniences.

Whenever left untreated, complexities can incorporate:

Weight gain or misfortune
actual agony
Substance use jumble
fits of anxiety
Relationship issues
Social disengagement
Contemplations of self destruction
Self-hurt
Eased back thinking or development
Exhaustion or low energy most days
Sensations of uselessness or responsibility
Loss of fixation or hesitation.

Kinds Of Depression

Melancholy can be broken into classes relying upon the seriousness of side effects. Certain individuals experience gentle and impermanent episodes, while others experience extreme and continuous burdensome episodes. There are two fundamental sorts: significant burdensome issue and industrious burdensome problem.

Significant Depressive Disorder:
Significant burdensome problem (MDD) is the more extreme type of discouragement. It's portrayed by persevering sensations of misery, sadness, and uselessness that don't disappear all alone and it is now and again called significant melancholy or clinical sorrow, unipolar discouragement

or essentially 'wretchedness'. What's more, it likewise includes loss of interest and joy in regular exercises, as well as different side effects as referenced. The side effects are capable most days and keep going for no less than about fourteen days. Side effects of sadness disrupt all region of an individual's life, including work and social connections.

There are different subtypes of significant burdensome issue these incorporate

Restless pain
Blended highlights
Peripartum beginning, during Pregnancy or just in the wake of Conceiving an offspring
Occasional examples
Melancholic elements
Insane elements
Mental shock

Constant Depressive Disorder:

Tenacious burdensome problem (PDD) used to be called dysthymia. It's a milder, however constant, type of despondency. For the determination to be made, side effects should keep going for no less than 2 years. PDD can influence your life more than significant sorrow since it goes on for a more drawn out period.

Side effects during a burdensome episode last consistently for the majority of the day and can keep going for a few days or weeks.

It's normal for individuals with PDD to:

Lose interest in typical day to day exercises

Feel miserable

Need efficiency

Have low confidence

Sorrow can be dealt with effectively, yet it's critical to adhere to your treatment plan.

There are additionally various kinds of burdensome issues. Side effects can go from generally minor (yet debilitating) through to exceptionally extreme, so it's useful to know about the scope of conditions and their particular side effects.

Different Types are;

Despondency: This is the term used to portray a serious type of wretchedness where large numbers of the actual side effects of misery are available. One of the significant changes is that the individual begins to move all the more leisurely. They're likewise bound to have a discouraged state of mind that is described by complete loss of delight in all things, or nearly everything.

Maniacal Depression

In some cases individuals with a burdensome issue can become really distracted and experience psychosis. This can include mental trips (seeing or hearing things that aren't there) or daydreams (deceptions that aren't shared by others, for example, accepting they are terrible or fiendishness, or that they're being watched or followed. They can likewise be jumpy, feeling like everybody is against them or that they are the reason for ailment or awful occasions happening around them.

Antenatal And Postnatal Depression:

Ladies are at an expanded gamble of discouragement during pregnancy (known as the antenatal or pre-birth period) and soon after labor (known as the post pregnancy period). You may likewise run over the term 'perinatal', which portrays the period covered by pregnancy and the main year after the child's introduction to the world.

The reasons for discouragement right now can be complicated and are many times the consequence of a blend of variables. In the days promptly following birth, numerous ladies experience the 'blue eyes' which is a typical condition connected with hormonal changes and influences up to 80 percent of ladies. The 'blue eyes', or general pressure acclimating to pregnancy as well as another child, are normal encounters, yet are not the same as misery. Wretchedness is longer enduring and can influence the mother, yet her relationship with her child, the youngster's turn of events, the mother's relationship with her accomplice and with different individuals from the family. Very nearly 10% of ladies will encounter gloom during pregnancy. This increments to 16 percent in the initial three months in the wake of having a child.

Bipolar Disorder: Bipolar confusion is by all accounts generally firmly connected to family ancestry. Stress and struggle can set off episodes for individuals with this condition and it's normal for bipolar confusion to be misdiagnosed as melancholy, liquor or substance addiction, consideration shortfall hyperactivity jumble (ADHD) or schizophrenia.

Conclusion relies upon the individual having had an episode of insanity and, except if noticed, this can be difficult to pick. It is entirely expected for individuals to go for quite a long time prior to getting an exact finding of bipolar problem. Assuming you're encountering ups and downs, making this unmistakable to your PCP or treating wellbeing professional is useful. Bipolar turmoil influences roughly 2% of the populace.

Bipolar discouragement happens in particular kinds of bipolar problem when an individual encounters a burdensome episode. Bipolar confusion is a psychological problem that causes particular changes in mind-set, energy, focus, and the capacity to do your everyday errands.

There are two sorts of bipolar problem, all of which incorporate periods known as hyper episodes, where you feel very "up," thrilled, or empowered, and burdensome episodes where you feel "down," miserable, or irredeemable.

Bipolar confusion utilized is additionally used to be known as 'hyper gloom' on the grounds that the individual encounters times of despondency and times of madness, with times of typical state of in the middle between.

Craziness resembles something contrary to melancholy and can differ in power - side effects incorporate inclination extraordinary, having loads of energy, having hustling considerations and little requirement for rest, talking rapidly, experiencing issues zeroing in on assignments, and feeling baffled and bad tempered. This isn't simply a momentary encounter. At times the individual becomes really distracted and has episodes of psychosis. Encountering psychosis includes pipedreams (seeing or hearing something not there) or having hallucinations (for example the individual accepting the person has superpowers). Assuming you have bipolar turmoil, perceiving the destructive impacts of every "mood can be hard". Assuming that bipolar problem is dealt with, many will encounter less and less serious side effects of gloom, assuming that they experience burdensome episodes.

7 Treatments That May Help Ease Symptoms Of Bipolar Depression.

Sorrow and Anxiety: Sorrow and tension can happen in an individual simultaneously. Truth be told, research has shown that more than 70 percentTrusted Source of individuals with burdensome issues additionally have side effects of nervousness.

However they're believed to be brought about by various things, sorrow and tension can deliver a few comparable side effects, which can include:

Touchiness
Trouble with memory or focus
rest issues
The two circumstances additionally share a few normal medicines.

Both tension and sadness can be treated
with
Treatment, as mental conduct treatment
Prescription
elective treatments, including
hypnotherapy

Cyclothymic Turmoil

Cyclothymic confusion is many times depicted as a milder type of bipolar problem. The individual encounters constant fluctuating mind-sets over no less than two years, including times of hypomania (a gentle to direct even out of lunacy) and times of burdensome side effects, with extremely brief periods (something like two months) of ordinariness between. The length of the side effects are more limited, less serious and not as standard, and in this way don't fit the models of bipolar problem or significant discouragement.

Dysthymic Jumble

The side effects of dysthymia are like those of significant melancholy yet are less extreme. Nonetheless, on account of dysthymia, side effects last longer. An individual must have this milder discouragement for over two years to be determined to have dysthymia.

Occasional Full Of Feeling Problem (SAD)

Miserable is a state of mind problem that has an occasional example. The reason for the problem is muddled, yet being connected with the variety in light openness in various seasons is thought. It's portrayed by mind-set unsettling influences (either times of wretchedness or lunacy) that start and end in a specific season. Gloom what begins in winter and dies down when the season closes is the most well-known. It's generally analyzed after the individual has had similar side effects during winter for several years. Individuals with SAD melancholy are bound to encounter an absence of energy, rest excessively, gorge, put on weight and pine for starches. Miserable is exceptionally uncommon in Australia and bound to be tracked down in nations with more limited days and longer times of obscurity, like in the chilly environment region of the Northern Hemisphere.

Melancholy and Fanatical Impulsive Problem (OCD)

Over the top urgent problem (OCD) is a sort of uneasiness problem. It causes undesirable and rehashed contemplations, desires, and fears (fixations).

These feelings of trepidation make you carry on rehashed ways of behaving or ceremonies (impulses) that you trust will facilitate the pressure brought about by the fixations. Individuals determined to have OCD habitually wind up in a circle of fixations and impulses. Assuming that you have these ways of behaving, you might feel disengaged as a result of them. This can prompt withdrawal from companions and social circumstances, which can expand your gamble for sorrow.

It's normal for somebody with OCD to likewise have melancholy. Having one tension problem can expand your chances for having another. Up to 80 percent of individuals with OCD additionally have significant sorrow episodes.

This double finding is a worry with youngsters, as well. Their enthusiastic ways of behaving, which might be first creating very early in life, can cause them to feel uncommon. That can prompt pulling out from companions and can build the opportunity of a youngster creating discouragement.
Treatment for despondency during pregnancy might zero in totally on talk treatment and other normal medicines. While certain ladies in all actuality do take antidepressants during their pregnancy, it's not satisfactory which ones are the most secure. Your medical care supplier might urge you to attempt an elective choice until after the introduction of your child.

The dangers for sadness can go on after the child shows up. Post birth anxiety, which is likewise called significant burdensome problem with peripartum beginning, is a serious worry for new moms. Perceiving the side effects might assist you with detecting an issue and look for help before it becomes overpowering.

Melancholy and Liquor
Research has laid out a connection between liquor use and melancholy. Individuals who have discouragement are bound to abuse liquor.
Drinking liquor every now and again can exacerbate side effects, and individuals who have misery are bound to abuse liquor or become subject to it.

Part 6.

FORESTALLING DEPRESSION

Gloom isn't by and large viewed as preventable. It's difficult to perceive what causes it, and that implies forestalling it is more troublesome. However, whenever you've encountered a burdensome episode, you might be more ready to forestall a future episode by realizing which way of life changes and medicines are useful.

Strategies That Might Help Include:

Standard activity
Getting a lot of rest
Keeping up with medicines
Diminishing pressure

Building solid associations with others Different methods and thoughts may likewise assist you with forestalling depression.

Things People With High-Functioning Depression Want You To Know

Spotting somebody with advanced depression can be troublesome. That is on the grounds that they frequently show up totally fine outwardly.

Losing Friends When You Have Depression

Everybody manages companion separations. However, the blow of losing a dear companion while managing sorrow felt a lot...

At-Home Ketamine Therapy:
At-home ketamine treatment is a protected and successful method for easing side effects related with nervousness and sorrow.

Perceiving Vegetative Symptoms of Depression

Vegetative side effects allude to the more actual changes brought about by melancholy. This incorporates inconvenience dozing, low energy levels, and center issues.

Unloading The Complex Link Between Depression And Substance Use

Sadness might raise your gamble for substance use issues — however substance use can likewise have an impact in despondency.

Conquering discouragement, it assists with knowing current realities

Depression is an ailment and not "sluggishness" or an impermanent reaction to typical despondency as well as debilitation.
It's memorable's critical that not every person who is discouraged is self-destructive. You can in any case look for help regardless of whether you haven't exhibited a particular self-destructive or self-hurt ways of behaving, or regardless of whether your side effects aren't quite as extreme or persevering as the side effects noted previously.

Alright, I'm feeling discouraged... so what's going on?

Now that you know the side effects of gloom, some sure adapting abilities can be valuable. For the accompanying strategies are all upheld by logical exploration and prescription prescribers — like specialists — and these abilities are regularly suggested as significant pieces of treatment in any event, for patients who keep on taking upper meds.

Practice These Adapting Abilities Consistently

I suggest doing numerous while perhaps not all of the accompanying adapting abilities and methods once per day while encountering despondency. It's critical to realize you likely won't be roused to do any of them at first since misery much of the time saps inspiration.

The Seven(7) Strategies Are:

1. Importance: View little ways as of administration to other people.
Find individual significance by serving an option that could be bigger than yourself. Recollect administration doesn't need to be huge to count. Think about this, "Achievement, similar to bliss, can't be sought after; it should result... as the accidental symptom of one's very own commitment to a course more significant than oneself.

2. Your objectives: Track down serviceable objectives that provide you with a feeling of achievement.

A great many people feel remorseful while discussing objectives since they put forth irrational or unfeasible objectives. An objective is useful in the event that it's: Something you have some control over (i.e., it doesn't rely upon others) Sensible (i.e., not overpowering) Reasonable for you (not for another person) Quantifiable (i.e., you know whether it is finished or finishing) On the off chance that something turns out badly with your objective, embrace a "what might I at any point gain from this?" mentality (versus a critical, "for this reason I'm horrendous" demeanor). Additionally, be cautious while contrasting your advancement and others. We ordinarily contrast our greatest shortcoming and someone else's greatest strength. This is unreasonable (and typically not precise at any rate).

3. Charming Occasions: Timetable lovely exercises or occasions.

Try not to hang tight for yourself to be "in that frame of mind." For instance, give yourself consent briefly "excursion" or timetable a solid leisure activity consistently. Simply make sure to do these exercises with the right disposition (see Commitment). Additionally, practice appreciation — set aside some margin to see what went well today, not exactly what turned out badly. Think about keeping an appreciation diary. Know that being thankful for your endowments doesn't mean you need to limit your concerns.

4. Commitment: Remain in the present. This training is once in a while called care. Decently well, during exercises make an effort not to be in that frame of mind with self-judgment. You will be unable to switch off the self-judgment, yet you can see it and take yourself delicately back to the present. Research shows that individuals with higher self-sympathy additionally have higher self-esteem or fearlessness.

For the individuals who experience issues with self-empathy or sound commitment, you can find self-sympathy practices on Kristin D. Neff's site here. Care Based Stress decrease courses are likewise accessible all through Utah.

5. Work out: And, eat right as well. Doing direct activity around five times each week (30 minutes a pop) can emphatically help your state of mind. Moderate activity is a degree of movement where it is hard to sing from your stomach while getting it done. Likewise focus on what the sort of food or drink you're eating means for your state of mind. You don't need to do craze eats less carbs, however anybody will be discouraged assuming they often gorge on carbs, unhealthy food, and caffeinated drinks. Recollect the prudence of balance.

6. Connections: Focus on individuals who lift you up.
Collaborate regularly with others that bring you up (not individuals that cut you down). While it's OK to have some alone time, track down an equilibrium and don't confine yourself or the downturn will wait.

7. Rest Regularly: Try to keep an ordinary rest plan.
Keep an equilibrium with not excessively little and not a lot of rest. Keeping awake until late one evening and afterward snoozing unreasonably the following day is a certain fire method for taking care of sorrow. Additionally, don't attempt to take care of issues late around evening time when your mind is extremely drowsy.

As you practice these adapting abilities, know that you're on the way to conquering depression.

Conversely, misery will in general wait when patients make up a motivation behind why they can't do these things. Regardless of what prescription you're taking, doing a few of these exercises consistently — particularly when you don't feel like it — is fundamental to the treatment of despondency. These positive adapting abilities might take time and practice, yet in the event that we don't require some investment to be well now, the times of "unwellness" might be constrained upon us later.

Depression Treatment

Treatment, medicine, self improvement? Assuming you're befuddled by all the different treatment choices for discouragement, this is the way to choose the best methodology for you.

Lady in specialist's office, leaning back in love seat as she checks out and cautiously pays attention to him. Tracking down the best wretchedness treatment for you when you're discouraged, it can feel like you won't ever get free from a dull shadow. Notwithstanding, even the most serious misery is treatable. In this way, on the off chance that your downturn is holding you back from carrying on with the existence you need to, go ahead and help. From treatment to medicine to solid way of life changes, there are a wide range of treatment choices accessible.

Obviously, similarly as no two individuals are impacted by wretchedness in the very same manner, nor is there a "one size fits all" treatment to fix sorrow. What works for one individual probably won't work for another. By becoming as educated as could be expected, however, you can find the medicines that can assist you with conquering sorrow, feel cheerful and confident once more, and recover your life.
of conversing with somebody eye to eye can be a gigantic assistance.

1. **Treatment takes time and responsibility**: These downturn medicines take time, and some of the time it could feel overpowering or frustratingly slow. That is typical. Recuperation normally has its high points and low points.

2. **Way of life changes:** A fundamental piece of despondency treatment
Way of life changes are straightforward yet amazing assets in the treatment of wretchedness. At times they may be all you really want. Regardless of whether you really want other treatment also, making the right way of life changes can assist with lifting sorrow quicker and keep it from returning.

3. **Way of life changes to treat gloom work out:** Standard activity can be as successful at regarding gloom as prescription. Besides the fact that exercise supports serotonin, endorphins, and other warm hearted cerebrum synthetic compounds, it sets off the development of new synapses and associations, very much like antidepressants

do. The best part is that you don't need to prepare for a long distance race to receive the rewards. Indeed, even a half-hour day to day walk can have a major effect. For greatest outcomes, go for the gold an hour of high-impact action as a general rule.

4. Social **help:** Solid interpersonal organizations diminish disconnection, a key gamble factor for wretchedness. Stay in touch with loved ones, or think about joining a class or gathering. Chipping in is a great method for getting social help and help other people while likewise helping yourself.

5. Nourishment Eating great is significant for both your physical and emotional well-being. Eating

little, even feasts over the course of the day will assist you with keeping your energy up and limit state of mind swings. While you might be attracted to sweet food varieties for the fast lift they give, complex carbs are a superior decision. They'll get you moving without the all-too early sugar crash.

6. **Rest emphatically affects temperament:** At the point when you don't get sufficient rest, your downturn side effects will be more awful. Lack of sleep compounds crabbiness, testiness, bitterness, and weakness. Ensure you're getting sufficient rest every evening. Not very many individuals excel on under seven hours per night. Go for the gold seven to nine hours every evening.

7. **Stress decrease** : Make changes in your day to day existence to help oversee and lessen pressure. An excess of stress fuels discouragement and endangers you for future melancholy. Take the parts of your life that worry you, for example, work over-burden or unsupportive connections, and track down approaches to minimize

Treatment and "the 10,000 foot view" in despondency treatment

One of the signs of discouragement is feeling overpowered and experiencing difficulty centering. Treatment helps you step back and see what may be adding to your downturn and how you can make changes.

8. **Connections:** figuring out the examples of your connections, fabricating better connections, and further developing current connections will assist with diminishing separation and construct social help, significant in forestalling melancholy.

9. **Defining sound limits:** Assuming that you are focused on and overpowered, and feel like you can't say no, you are more in danger for wretchedness. Defining sound limits in connections and at work can assist with easing pressure, and treatment can help you distinguish and approve the limits that are ideal for you.

10. **Taking care of life's concerns:** Chatting with a believed specialist can give great input on additional positive ways of taking care of life's difficulties and issues.

Individual or gathering treatment, at the point when you hear "treatment" you could naturally imagine one-on-one meetings with a specialist. Nonetheless, bunch treatment can be exceptionally helpful in sadness treatment also. Both gathering and individual treatment meetings generally last about 60 minutes. What are the advantages of each? In individual treatment, you are building serious areas of strength for a with one individual, and may feel more open to imparting a delicate data to one individual than with a gathering. You additionally stand out.

In bunch treatment, paying attention to peers going through similar battles can approve your encounters and assist with building confidence. Frequently bunch individuals are at various places in their downturn, so you could get tips from both somebody down and dirty and somebody who has taken care of through a difficult issue. As well as giving motivation and suggestions, going to bunch treatment can likewise assist with expanding your social exercises and organization.

Whenever hardship rears its ugly head in treatment...
As with redesigning a house, when you dismantle things that haven't functioned admirably in your life, it frequently exacerbates them before they improve. At the point when treatment appears to be troublesome or difficult, don't surrender. Assuming that you examine your sentiments and responses genuinely with your advisor, it will assist you with

pushing ahead instead of retreat back to your old, less viable ways.

Notwithstanding, on the off chance that the association with your specialist reliably begins to feel constrained or awkward, don't hesitate for even a moment to investigate different choices for treatment too. A solid believing relationship is the underpinning of good treatment.

Tracking down a specialist
One of the main interesting points while picking a specialist is your association with this individual. The right specialist will be a mindful and strong accomplice in your downturn treatment and recuperation.

There are numerous ways of tracking down a specialist:

Informal exchange is one of the most mind-blowing ways of tracking down a decent specialist. Your loved ones might have a few thoughts, or your essential consideration specialist might have the option to give an underlying reference. Public psychological wellness associations can likewise assist with reference arrangements of authorized credentialed suppliers.
Assuming expense is an issue, look at nearby senior habitats, strict associations, and local area emotional well-being facilities. Such puts frequently offer treatment on a sliding scale for installment.
Drug for despondency
Melancholy medicine might be the most promoted treatment for sorrow, however

that doesn't mean it is the best. Wretchedness isn't just about a compound unevenness in the mind. Prescription might assist with letting some free from the side effects of moderate and extreme discouragement, yet it doesn't fix the hidden issue, and it's normally not a drawn out arrangement. Upper drugs likewise accompany aftereffects and security concerns, and withdrawal can be truly challenging. Assuming you're thinking about whether stimulant drug is appropriate for you, realizing the real factors can assist you with settling on an educated choice.

Regardless of whether you choose to take drug for discouragement, don't disregard different medicines. Way of life changes and treatment assist with speeding recuperation from wretchedness, yet additionally give abilities to assist with forestalling a repeat.

TMS treatment for despondency
Assuming you're experiencing significant sadness that has been impervious to treatment, drug, and self improvement, then, at that point, TMS treatment might be a choice. Transcranial attractive feeling (TMS) treatment is a harmless treatment that coordinates repeating attractive energy beats at the locales of the mind that are engaged with temperament. These attractive heartbeats go effortlessly through the skull and invigorate synapses which can further develop correspondence between various pieces of the cerebrum and straightforwardness wretchedness side effects.

While TMS might have the option to further develop treatment-safe melancholy, that doesn't mean it's a remedy for misery or that your side effects won't return. Notwithstanding, it could give adequate enhancements in your energy and drive to empower you to start talk treatment or make the way of life changes — like working on your eating routine, working out, and constructing your encouraging group of people — that can assist with saving your downturn recuperation in the long haul.

Option and correlative medicines
Option and correlative medicines for despondency might incorporate nutrient and home grown enhancements, needle therapy, and unwinding methods, like care contemplation, yoga, or jujitsu.

Nutrients And Enhancements For misery
The jury is still out on how well home grown cures, nutrients, or enhancements work in treating sorrow. While many enhancements are broadly available without a prescription, by and large their viability has not been deductively demonstrated. On the off chance that your

downturn side effects are to some extent because of nourishing lack, you might profit from nutrient enhancements, however this ought to be on the counsel of your medical services proficient.

Assuming you choose to attempt normal and natural enhancements, recall that they can make side impacts and medication or food cooperations. For instance, St. John's Wort — a promising spice utilized for treatment of gentle to direct melancholy — can obstruct physician recommended medications, for example, blood thinners, contraception pills, and medicine antidepressants. Ensure your primary care physician or specialist understands what you are taking.

Other elective medicines
Unwinding procedures. As well as assisting with freeing side effects from discouragement, unwinding methods may likewise decrease pressure and lift sensations of delight and prosperity. Attempt yoga, profound breathing,

moderate muscle unwinding, or contemplation.

Needle therapy. Needle therapy, the procedure of involving fine needles on unambiguous focuses on the body for remedial intentions, is progressively being examined as a treatment for melancholy, with some examination concentrates on showing promising outcomes. Assuming that you choose to attempt needle therapy, ensure that you view as an authorized qualified proficient.

here are many kinds of treatment accessible. Three of the more normal techniques utilized in discouragement treatment incorporate mental social treatment, relational treatment, and psychodynamic treatment. Frequently, a mixed methodology is utilized.

Occasional full of feeling issue (Miserable)

Miserable is a mind-set jumble that has an occasional example. The reason for the problem is hazy, however being connected with the variety in light openness in various seasons is thought. It's described by state of mind unsettling influences (either times of sorrow or craziness) that start and end in a specific season.

Melancholy what begins in winter and dies down when the season closes is the most well-known. It's typically analyzed after the individual has had similar side effects during winter for several years. Individuals with gloom are bound to encounter an absence of energy, rest excessively, gorge, put on weight and pine for sugars. Miserable is exceptionally uncommon in Australia and bound to be tracked down in nations with more limited days and longer times of obscurity, like in the chilly environment region of the Northern Side of the equator.

Conclusion

Depression can be transitory, or it tends to be a drawn out challenge. Treatment doesn't necessarily in all cases make your downturn disappear totally.
Be that as it may, treatment frequently makes side effects more sensible. Overseeing side effects of sadness includes tracking down the right blend of meds and treatments.
In the event that one treatment doesn't work, talk with your medical services proficient. They can assist you with making an alternate treatment plan that might work better in assisting you with dealing with your condition. Keep in mind, discouragement is treatable and viable medicines are accessible. The previous you look for help, the better for you.

www.ingramcontent.com/pod-product-compliance
Lightning Source LLC
Chambersburg PA
CBHW071338140726
47996CB00005B/2036